Friendship & Forgiveness
Harley And His Wheelchair

BRENT POPPEN

Playground Lessons– Friendship and Forgiveness
Harley and His Wheelchair By Brent Poppen

Published By

SelfPublishing.com
Helping Authors Become Publishers

Illustrations, design and layout by
JohnsonMEDIA**Group**
CAYMAN ISLANDS
www.johnsonmedia-group.com

Printed in the United States of America
ISBN-10: 1475035179
ISBN-13: 9781475035179
First Edition printed 2012

Contents

Dedication

This book is dedicated to all the Mrs. Poppens who have found their path in teaching and are leading our children to a brighter future. Thank you!

Love,
Brent Poppen

Acknowledgements

I extend my deepest gratitude to:

Erika, my wife, your unconditional love has changed my life forever. A day never goes by that I do not remember how blessed I am that you are the love of my life.

Sam and Jackie Poppen, Dad and Mom, your enduring spirit of support never goes unnoticed.

Mandy "Pookie" Poppen, my sister, you have my back unconditionally which allows me to do more in life than I could ever imagine.

Gary and Carol Peters, my in-laws, thanks for all the kindness you share with me.

Marci Garcia, thank you for planting a seed to make this book possible. Your "mijo" did it.

My Long Beach, California family, your friendship and love makes each new day become a day to cherish.

Dr. Lucile Richardson, our paths were meant to cross after twenty one years. Thanks for your guidance and lighting a path for my autobiography. I will never forget that first email.

Preface

This children's book came to life as a result of a blood infection in July 2010, which came close to ending my life. I was hospitalized and spent twenty-three days in the intensive care unit. I received twelve weeks of multiple IV antibiotics while at home, and spent several months on bed rest almost twenty four hours a day.

While those were the hardest months of my life, I now can say that I am thankful for the time to reflect on God's mercy towards me. I am a living testimony! Thanks to all my family, friends, teachers and students who have helped me in staying on my journey.

Introduction

A sports accident at age sixteen caused a spinal-cord injury that left me paralyzed for life. I became a quadriplegic, losing complete use of my legs with some paralysis in my upper extremities.

I have spent several years speaking and teaching in schools. Being disabled creates discussion issues specific to the students and their involvement with me. They learn about self-confidence, patience, sacrifice and determination along with many other life and educational topics. I believe education and open discussions will change minds and hearts. This is the path to creating acceptance.

PLAYGROUND LESSONS: FRIENDSHIP AND FORGIVENESS is a story about a little boy named Harley and his wheelchair. The story contains many emotional issues that I had and still deal with on a daily basis. These include: ignorance, bullying, and being a leader.

This short story is designed to be read to, or by students, in different grade levels, while creating meaningful discussions and lessons.

SECTION 1

FEAR · ANXIETY · COMPASSION
Harley Starts Second Grade

Should physical differences in appearance affect how you treat someone else?

Harley's First Day of School

Harley wakes up for his first day of Second Grade at his new school. Staring at his wheelchair next to his bed, he talks to it like it might be his only friend today. Telling it,

"I am afraid that the teachers and children are not going to be nice to me. They will make fun of me because I look different. I will be the only child in a wheelchair at school."

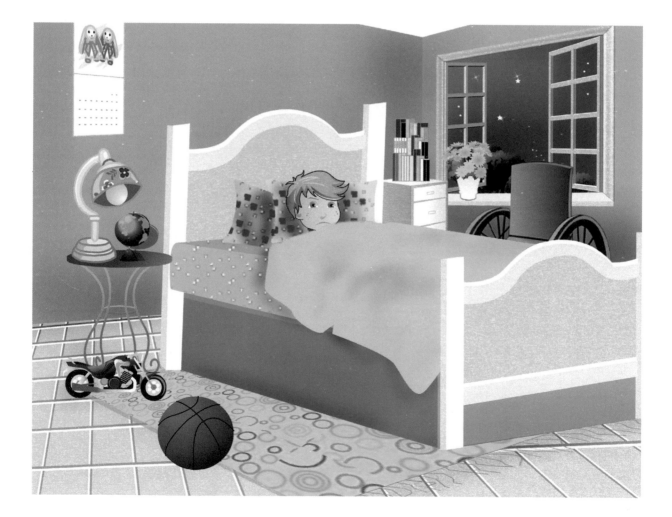

The Bus Stop

Harley gets dressed in his school colors and puts on his favorite yellow checkered shoes. His mom pours him a yummy bowl of frosted cereal, and minutes later both walk down to the bus stop. This is where he will be picked up and dropped off from his school. It is where his mom will be waiting with a big hug when she asks how he enjoyed his first day.

Harley Hears Whispers

Harley and his mom are nervous as they see the huge yellow bus coming down the street. They both can hear the other children quietly asking their parents,

"Why is he in that wheelchair?"

"Is he hurt?" And,

"What's wrong with his legs?"

Harley wants to turn around and answer their questions to let them know he can hear them. The bus is pulling up to the curb. Harley and his mom hope the bus has a wheelchair lift so he can ride to school with the other children.

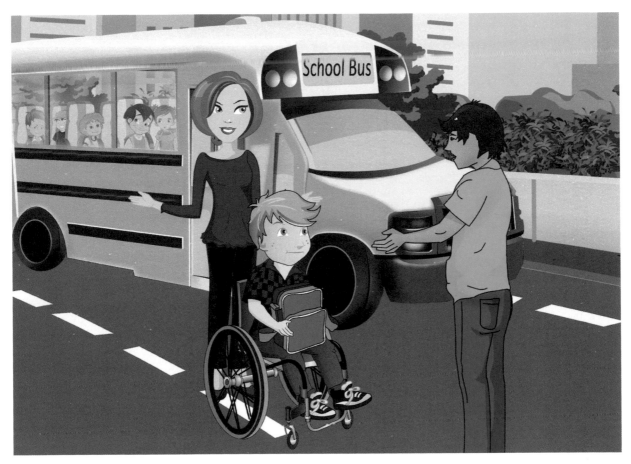

Harley and the School Bus

The bus stops as the brakes make a loud screeching noise and the tall skinny door swings open. The children hug their parents and run onto the bus, each trying to get a window seat to wave goodbye. As the last child steps onto the bus, the driver sees Harley and his mom. Harley has seen this look before. It is the look of being nervous and ashamed all at the same time. Harley knows he will not get on that school bus even before the bus driver says,

"I am sorry but you cannot ride this bus."

The driver turns to Harley's mom,

"You will need to call the school and request a bus with a lift."

Harley watches all the children as they ride the bus to their first day of school.

Classroom 209

Harley and his mom hold hands as they walk back home. She will be taking her son with his wheelchair to his first day of Second Grade at his new school. The school bell rings as she parks the car in front of the school. Harley leaps into his wheelchair. He swings his new backpack over the back of his wheelchair and races to Classroom 209. He leaves his mom far in the distance, but she follows him just to make sure he is okay.

Harley Meets His Teacher

As Harley grabs the classroom door, he sees his mom leaving the school. He takes a nervous breath knowing what is about to happen as he opens the door. Harley swings the heavy door open and pushes his wheelchair into his classroom. Just like he thought, there was a room full of students staring at him. Before any child could whisper or yell,

"What is wrong with you?"

"Why do you have a wheelchair?" the pretty teacher named Mrs. Poppen greets Harley with a big smile and hug,

"Welcome to Second Grade. You must be Harley; I have been waiting for you. One of your classmates told me that a boy in a wheelchair could not get on the bus because there was no wheelchair lift to hold his wheelchair. I was hoping that was you."

Harley also recognized some of the children from the bus stop.

7

Harley's Mom Watches From The Window

Harley quickly feels welcomed to his classroom. Mrs. Poppen has a desk ready with his name tag hanging on the front. There are also pencils and crayons neatly placed in his pencil box. She has already removed the chair so Harley could roll his wheelchair right up to it. Mrs. Poppen introduces herself and goes over the class rules, explaining that Classroom 209 is a family. She wants the students to know what is expected from them and what they can expect from her.

On the outside of the classroom are the eyes of a loving mother looking through the window that only the teacher sees. It is not the first pair of eyes that Harley's teacher has seen peeping on the first day of school. She smiles and appreciates a mom's concern for her son.

The first recess bell will soon ring and Harley starts to feel nervous, again. He wishes he did not have to go outside for recess; instead he could just stay in the room all day with his teacher.

LONELINESS · ACCEPTANCE

Harley Pushes On
The Playground

Is it right that Harley wants to be treated like everyone else? Why?

Harley Pushes Himself Around The Playground

Harley is last to leave the classroom. He sits staring at a huge playground filled with children. Some are playing with balls, some are just running around and others are on the slides. Harley thinks he should just push his wheelchair around to see whether anyone would ask him to play. He pushes by the kickball courts, basketball courts and handball wall, and no one asks if he wants to play. Harley feels like he has pushed for miles. He knows he could do most of the playground games, although the other children might not think he can.

Harley Just Wants To Play

Harley has played kickball, basketball and handball games at home with his family for as long as he could remember. There he was treated the same as his older brothers. When they played basketball in the driveway, handball against the garage, or chalked out a four square on the sidewalk, they made sure Harley could play along in his wheelchair. Sometimes, he played well and could almost beat his older brothers. He feels the children will never allow him to play. All Harley wants is to be like the other children and just play!

Harley's First Day Of School Is Over

As the last bell rings at 2:30 p.m., all the children run out of the room with their backpacks swinging in the air. Harley makes sure he is last to leave. He loves his classroom. Harley feels comfortable inside the room knowing that Mrs. Poppen went out of her way to make sure it was ready for him and his wheelchair. He hugs her goodbye and says,

"Thank you Mrs. Poppen for making all of us feel so special today."

Harley Is A Good Athlete

Harley and his teacher open the door to find his mom waiting outside with a big smile on her face. His mom asks Harley to wait on the sidewalk near their car as she speaks privately with Mrs. Poppen. His teacher explains to his mom that Harley was great in the classroom, but she noticed how he pushed his wheelchair around the playground without playing with other children.

"My son is a good athlete and could play most of the games on the playground. Maybe the children do not know how to play with him because they do not know what he can do in his wheelchair. Probably it is their first time being around a child in a wheelchair," explained Harley's mom.

Mrs. Poppen also did not know what Harley was able to do on the playground. She left school thinking about ways that she could help him feel accepted by the other children during their play time.

INDEPENDENCE • EQUALITY
Harley Plays Basketball

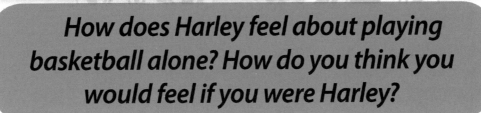

How does Harley feel about playing basketball alone? How do you think you would feel if you were Harley?

Harley's Second Day Of School

Harley wakes up for his second day of school. Again staring at his wheelchair, Harley thinks to himself,

"I feel nervous. I want to hurry and get into my classroom."

That is where he feels safe and accepted.

"I will be taking you to school until they get a bus with a lift," says Harley's mom.

Harley is good at being patient. He is still sad about not being able to ride the school bus with the other children. Harley does not know that his mom is already working hard to make this happen.

Harley Shows Independence

Today Harley's mom stays in the car and allows her son to roll his wheelchair to his classroom alone. Harley likes showing others he can do many things without their help.

The bell rings and the children line up to enter the class. Harley makes sure he is first in line. He pushes a little faster when everyone is close so he can hold the door open for his teacher and classmates. That catches Mrs. Poppen by surprise. The other children think it is cool that Harley can do this. They say "Thank you," as they enter the room. Harley knows he has to show his classmates that he can be just like them in and outside the classroom.

Harley On The Huge Playground

Harley is having a great day at school. He has made a few friends in his class. Harley watches the clock. He sees that it is almost time for morning recess and starts to get that funny feeling in his stomach. Harley must leave his classroom and push his wheelchair onto that huge playground just like he did on the first day of school. When the bell rings, Harley, like always, is last to leave his desk. He watches all the children scatter to their playground areas. Harley always wonders how they know where to go and play without asking each other.

Harley Plays Basketball Alone

Harley pushes his wheelchair out and onto an open basketball court which was not crowded. He pushes around following all the painted lines on the ground. Harley thinks that he is a famous basketball player shooting the ball and making almost every shot go into the basket. He hears all the children yelling, laughing, and having fun. Harley also wants to yell and laugh.

Harley Wants To Be Treated The Same As Others

In Harley's mind he can see himself throwing up a ball to win his game. In the distance, he notices a lady walking towards him. Harley is hoping that he is not in trouble for pushing his wheelchair too fast since it happened at his last school. He always wants to make it go faster because it is his way of running. Harley never sees the other children who can walk get into trouble for running too fast on the basketball court. He just wants to be treated the same even if he falls. It would not be his first or last tumble from his wheelchair to the ground! Harley just wants the other children to see him the same as they see each other.

Harley and His Teacher Playing Basketball

Coming closer to Harley on the playground is Mrs. Poppen. He knows there is more time left before the recess bell would ring. Harley thinks to himself,

"Why is she coming out to the basketball courts? What is she carrying behind her back?"

He pushes towards her. Mrs. Poppen with her usual big, pretty smile throws a basketball towards Harley. He is surprised and almost knocked backwards. Quickly Harley catches it with both hands.

"This feels like home," thinks Harley.

He throws it back to her as hard as possible. Catching the ball, Mrs. Poppen says,

"Harley, do you want to shoot some hoops with me?"

Excitedly, he replies "Yes, that would be great."

The Quiet Playground

Harley and his teacher are on the basketball court. He is enjoying making all the shots that Mrs. Poppen misses. She chases down Harley's air balls. Mrs. Poppen is surprised to see Harley pushing his wheelchair and dribbling the ball at the same time. He suddenly realizes that the playground is quiet. Harley can feel the children staring at him. They have never seen a teacher play a game with the students during recess. Harley knows this is a special day. He hopes the bell would never ring, but it does!

"This is now your special ball, Harley. You can take it from the room during every recess and lunch break," says Mrs. Poppen.

25

Harley Wins

The lunch bell comes fast. It is like magic. Harley wants to hurry back to the basketball court again because he had a fun time during the first recess. He knows exactly where Mrs. Poppen kept the basketball. When the bell rings, Harley quickly grabs the ball from the closet. Like always, he waits to be the last student leaving the room.

"Mind you Harley, no playing is allowed in the classroom or the ball will be locked away," says Mrs. Poppen.

Harley smiles as he leaves the room. He hurries to eat the lunch which he brought from home so he does not lose any time shooting hoops on the basketball court.

Harley takes the last bite from a peanut butter and jelly sandwich. He throws his trash in the garbage and races to the basketball courts. All the way there, he is dribbling or throwing the ball ahead and catching it on a single bounce.

"10, 9, 8, 7, 6, 5, 4, 3, 2, 1!" Harley shoots. He makes a loud buzzer sound as if he was in a real playoff game. He watches the ball circle around the basketball rim. His ball falls through the hoop in a slow motion, and Harley wins!

FRIENDSHIP • LIFE'S LESSONS

Harley Makes Friends

> *Why did Harley think that "winning" was not important on the basketball court?*

New Students On The Basketball Courts

Hearing footsteps behind him, Harley grins. Hoping that when he turns around, he will again see his teacher asking him to play basketball. Harley leans back holding the rims of his wheelchair. He causes the front wheels to come off the ground while swinging around. It's a "wheelie." Harley was creating room for the ball to go under the wheelchair without being touched. He was showing off! To his surprise, the children were standing behind him. Some were his classmates and some were from another second grade class. Harley was shocked!

"Why were these children on the court with me? Did they want my ball or did they want this court?"

It seemed like a long time before any words were spoken.

Harley Plays "HORSE"

Harley's classmates break the silence on the court.

"This is Harley."

"Hello. It is cool that you can play basketball in a wheelchair," the other second graders responded.

"Do you want to play basketball with me?" asked Harley.

His new friends were puzzled. Never before had they played basketball with a child in a wheelchair.

They decide to play a shooting game called "H.O.R.S.E." Each player must spell the word "horse" if they miss a shot.

Harley is happy to be playing with the other children on the playground.

Life's Lessons On The Basketball Court

When the lunch bell rings, three out of the six children still had not spelled the word "horse." Harley is one of those three still in the game, but he is almost out. He has spelled "H, O, R, and S." One more missed shot and Harley will be out. He could have been first to lose and it would have been okay with him. Winning was not important. It was all about playing with the other children.

Mrs. Poppen secretly spies on the basketball court. She sees all the children playing together and having fun. With a tear running down her cheek, Mrs. Poppen realizes these are lessons she could not teach in the classroom.

Just Another Second Grader

When playing basketball with his new friends, Harley was just another second grader. It was his best day in school! He was not thinking of himself as the only student in a wheelchair. Harley finally felt he was treated the same as all the children on that giant playground, just yelling, playing and laughing. He could not wait to share this day with his mom. He watches the clock from his desk and waits for the short hand to be on the "2" and the long hand on the "6." The bell rings and the students are excused. Harley waits to be the last student to leave. He gives his teacher a tight hug.

"Thank you for helping me make new friends."

Harley Tells A Story

Harley comes wheeling his chair around the corner in front of the school with his backpack over his shoulders. His mom sees a smile that she had not seen in a long time. Before she could open the car door, Harley waves goodbye to his new friends. He puts his wheelchair next to his mom's car and opens the car door, swinging himself into his seat. His mom puts the wheelchair in the trunk. Excited to tell her about his day, Harley could hardly speak clearly during the entire ride. His mom just smiled and allowed him to be excited. He finally got the whole story out as she pulled into the driveway. Mom had a smile almost as big as her son. Harley would never forget this day!

SECTION 5

BULLYING

Harley Plays Kickball

Is it right to judge people like the children on the kickball court did with Harley? What are the consequences of this behavior?

Harley Gets To School Early

Friday morning marks the end of Harley's best week of school. He loves his classroom and his desk. Harley loves his new friends, but he has a special love for his teacher, Mrs. Poppen.

He wakes up and stretches. Harley grabs his wheelchair and hurries to get ready so he could arrive at school early.

A few classmates are going to play basketball or kickball before school. They had asked if he wanted to play. Harley is hoping it would be basketball because he had already played this game with other children. He knows he can play kickball, but the other children had never seen him play that game. Harley thinks they might not choose him to be on their team.

Basketball Or Kickball

Harley's mom is happy to take her son to school early so he can play with his classmates. It makes her feel good knowing the children like him. She knows there may be times when he would not be as happy, but it is not now. All children have good and bad days at school. She knows this is a normal part of growing up.

Harley's mom turns the corner near the school. He sees that the basketball courts are empty and wonders whether the other children are there yet. Near the far corner of the playground, Harley sees a group of children at the kickball courts. Maybe Mrs. Poppen is already in her classroom and he can just stay in Room 209 until the bell rings.

Harley Checks His Classroom For Mrs. Poppen

Before heading to the kickball court, Harley pushes to his classroom to see whether the door is open. He grabs the door and it is locked. Still hoping, he sits on the edge of his wheelchair to look through the window.

"Please, please Mrs. Poppen, please be in the classroom."

She is not.

Now Harley's tummy is starting to hurt. He starts the long push out to the corner of the playground where the children are choosing kickball teams.

A Playground Bully

Harley arrives at the courts and sees two of his new friends. While they are coming over to say hi, he hears a bully say,

"Why is he here? He cannot walk. So how is he going to play?"

A few other children laugh at what is being said. Harley just wishes to be back on the basketball courts where he would be comfortable.

The bully also says,

"Wheelchairs should play with wheelchairs. Why are you at our school?"

Harley's friends turn to the bully. One of them replies,

"How is he going to play with other wheelchairs? He is the only one in a wheelchair….da! Harley can be on our team," the other friend replies.

Harley feels special because his friends are happy for him.

Harley Plays

Harley's team starts the kicking. The team in the field asks if everyone wants to play with a "two out" instead of the "three out" rule. This allows more innings to be played. All the children like this rule. His new friends tell him,

"You go first, Harley."

He goes close to the box near the home plate. There is a long pause. Harley was asked,

"How do you want the ball pitched? Some children like "baby bounces" and some like it rolled without bounces."

Harley says, "Give me big bounces. I can hit it with my hand instead of kicking it."

The children thought that was a cool idea, except one!

"If you cannot kick it, you should not be able to play," yelled the bully!

The other children want Harley to play, so the bully stops yelling at him

Homerun

Harley takes a huge swing as the ball comes bouncing towards the plate. The only place he does not want the ball to go to is second base. Of course, that was exactly where the ball went. The bully could have just thrown the ball to first base, but he would rather teach Harley a lesson. He runs directly toward Harley with the kickball, ready to throw it at him. Harley pushes up to first base because he is ready for this. The bully throws his arm back. Harley can see that he is aiming to hit the wheelchair. The ball flies fast in Harley's direction. He grabs his wheels, pulling back making another "wheelie" like the first time he was on the court. The children think Harley will get hit, but they are wrong. As Harley makes a "wheelie," the ball goes right under his wheelchair without touching him or the wheelchair. It goes so far that he is able to score a homerun. His team cheers for him as he pushes fast around all the bases.

Pitcher

After two "outs," they change sides. Harley is now in the field. He is the pitcher for his team. The first student lines up to kick. He thinks all he has to do is just kick the ball back to Harley and he would reach first base. How would Harley grab the ball from the ground in his wheelchair and be able to get the boy out? The runner is wrong. Harley lets the ball roll up on his wheel throwing it hard to first base. He beats the runner and gets him out. The children are amazed and quiet. The ball is never kicked back to Harley. The children learn quickly that Harley can play kickball.

SECTION 6

FORGIVENESS
Harley Teaches The "Golden Rule"

Did Harley do the right thing by helping the bully? Why?
What did you learn from Harley's story?

The Bully Gets Knocked Down

Harley was taught to be nice to others even if they are not nice to him. He wants to hit the bully with the ball before pitching it, but he also knows that would be wrong.

"How do you want the ball pitched? Baby bounces or rolled without bounces?"

"Give me the roll," replied the bully.

Harley rolls it to him. The bully wants to show off and get a home run. He kicks it as hard as he could and the ball goes far. The bully is able to get around all the bases. He heads for the home plate. Another student from Harley's team catches the ball. Turning around, he throws it towards the home plate. The bully is crossing the plate. The ball hits his legs, knocks him and sends him flying in the air. He lands hard yelling not just once, but many times, while holding his ankle, crying in pain!

The children feel the bully will be okay. Soon he will get up so they could finish the game. But it does not happen that way. The bully never stops crying! His ankle swells, turning red, then blue. The students know this is really bad.

It is too early in the morning, the children do not know what to do. There is no coach or teacher on the playground, and the nurse has not yet arrived at school.

Harley Gives The Bully A Ride

None of the children are strong enough to carry the bully, and walking is too painful for him! He cannot put any pressure on his ankle. A few children head to the office to get help. Harley does not like seeing the bully crying and in pain. Although they were not friends … yet, Harley was taught to help others because others have always helped him. Harley pushes over to home plate where the bully is still crying. He reaches out,

"I can help you get to the office."

Harley helps him stand on his good leg. The bully thinks, "Why would Harley want to help me?"

"Turn around and sit on my lap. I will push you all the way to the office!"

The children do not realize how strong Harley is until they see him roll the bully all the way to the office without stopping. It is a long ride there! Harley is hoping that someone will be in the office when they arrive.

Back To Room 209

The principal walks out of his office. A few children explain what has happened on the kickball courts. He could not believe his eyes. Harley is wheeling his chair all the way from the corner of the playground with the bully on his lap. Harley is breathing heavily. The bully still has tears running down his cheeks.

"Thank you, young man. You have done a magnificent job!" The principal takes the bully to the nurse's office.

"Hooray for Harley! Can we have rides too?" asked the children.

Harley replied with a big smile, "I am just a little bit tired."

Ring! Ring! Ring!

Everyone lines up to enter their classrooms.

Friendship Wins

Mrs. Poppen has already heard what happened on the kickball court from many of her students, but she has not heard from Harley.

"Thank you for being helpful to another student on the playground this morning. It is important to do the right thing even when others are not kind."

Before the lunch break, there is a knock on Mrs. Poppen's door. In walks the principal with the bully and his mom.

"Good morning, I have someone who would like to speak with the class."

The bully limps up to the front of the class on crutches. His ankle is in a cast.

"I am sorry for treating you different because you are in a wheelchair, Harley. I am also sorry for being a bully to all of you. Will you please sign my cast? You go first, Harley."

Harley goes up to the bully with a big grin on his face. He grabs the black pen and draws a picture of his wheelchair, then signs his name.

This was another day that Mrs. Poppen and many children would never forget!

ABOUT THE AUTHOR

Brent Poppen is an author, substitute teacher, counselor and an international motivational speaker. A sports accident at age sixteen caused a spinal-cord injury that left him paralyzed for life. Brent became a quadriplegic, losing complete use of his legs with some paralysis in his upper extremities. This was an ending in many ways, but also a beginning to journeys he never dreamed! His spinal-cord injury did not paralyze his athletic dreams, because he has become one of the top disabled athletes in the world. Brent competed in two consecutive Paralympics, Athens 2004 and Beijing 2008, in wheelchair rugby and tennis. He earned a Bronze Medal in wheelchair rugby and has received numerous Gold Medals and world titles in both sports.

Brent is also an avid water skier, teaching other disabled persons either at his home lake, or through his water ski programs with Children's Hospital in Fresno, California.

Poppen earned a bachelor's degree in social science from Chapman College in Southern California. He is a rehabilitation counselor at Children's Hospital in Fresno California. Poppen has served on staff at the Boys School (a youth correctional facility) in Paso Robles, California.

Brent and Erika met while college students and dated for several years before becoming happily married. They later moved from Long Beach to Paso Robles, California, where Brent does substitute teaching and Erika is an elementary school teacher.

For more information:
Website: www.booksbybrent.com
Email: poppenbrent@gmail.com
Tel: 805-801-8349

Also Available From Brent Poppen!!!
Tragedy On The Mountain
A Quadriplegic's Journey From Paralysis To Paralympics

Foreword By Baseball Legend, BOBBY GRICH

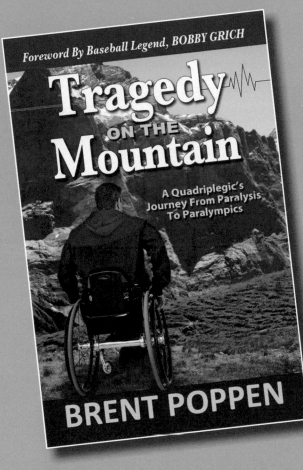

www.booksbybrent.com
Or call 805-801-8349

PLAY GROUND LESSONS

Friendship & Forgiveness

54

55

Made in the USA
Lexington, KY
09 November 2012